and the
PECULIAR PARCEL

For Orlando
J.S.

For Sally and Matty
C.E

Reading Consultant: Prue Goodwin, Lecturer in literacy and children's books

ORCHARD BOOKS
338 Euston Road, London NW1 3BH
Orchard Books Australia
Level 17/207 Kent Street, Sydney, NSW 2000

First published in 2012
First paperback publication in 2013

ISBN 978 1 40831 330 5 (hardback)
ISBN 978 1 40831 338 1 (paperback)

Text © Justine Smith 2012
Illustrations © Clare Elsom 2012

A CIP catalogue record for this book is available from the British Library.

1 3 5 7 9 10 8 6 4 2 (hardback)
1 3 5 7 9 10 8 6 4 2 (paperback)

Printed in China

Orchard Books is a division of Hachette Children's Books,
an Hachette UK company.

and the
PECULIAR PARCEL

Justine Smith • Clare Elsom

ORCHARD

Zak Zoo lives at Number One, Africa Avenue.
His mum and dad are away on
safari, so his animal family is looking
after him. Sometimes things get a little . . .

. . . WILD!

Emily

Pam

Dad

Mum

Zak

Nanny
Hilda

Petula

Bob

Charlie

Mia (Zak's best friend)

Ping

Zak Zoo was expecting a parcel today. But the postman drove past the house without stopping.

Zak called the post office. "Don't you have a parcel for me?" he asked.
"I do," said Percy. "But I can't be your postman any more."
"Why not?" asked Zak.

"It's too dangerous," said Percy.

"Last week your lions attacked me!"

"But they are just cubs," said Zak.

"They were only playing."

"Your buffalo bit me, too," said
Percy.

"He was just hungry," said Zak.

"He thought you were breakfast."

"And your bear squashed me!"
said Percy.

"I can explain," said Zak. "That
was a bear-hug. He likes you!"

Zak went to the post office. He decided not to take the lion cubs, the buffalo or the bear. He took Emily the elephant instead.

"Morning, Percy," said Zak. "Please may I have my parcel now?"

Percy saw Emily, and hid under the desk.

Zak got under the desk to talk to Percy.
"I think I'll get a new job," Percy told
Zak. "I'll open a cafe."
"What a good idea!" said Zak.

While Percy was talking to Zak,
Emily helped with the post.

"Percy is nice," Zak said as they left.
"But he is not a very good postman."

Emily agreed. She hoped Percy
would open his cafe.

Zak went home to open his parcel.
Inside there was a letter.

Camp Faraway
The Jungle
Dear Zak,   Africa

Here is a present for you.

Love,
Mum and Dad
X X X

P.S. Are you washing behind
your ears properly?

Zak's best friend Mia came over to
see the present.
"What is it?" asked Zak.

"It's a seed," guessed Mia.

Mia was right! Everyone helped
Zak plant the seed, and Emily
watered it.

The young plant grew very quickly.
It sprouted more leaves and flowers
every day.

"I think it's a girl plant,"
said Mia.

"Let's call her Gloria," said Zak.

Zak wrote to his parents.

Dear Mum and Dad,

Thank you for the hairy plant.
I'm going to call her Gloria.

Love, Zak

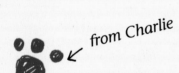
from Charlie

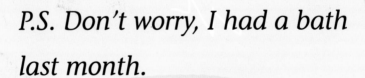

P.S. Don't worry, I had a bath
last month.

Soon Gloria started turning brown.
Nanny Hilda watered her every
day, but still her leaves curled up.

Everyone tried to feed Gloria, but
what did she want to eat?
She didn't like flies.

She didn't like worms, either.

Zak collected some buffalo poo.
"It's good for plants," said Zak.
"Yuk!" said Mia. She was taking the
gerbil to her house, in case Gloria
ate him.

Then Nanny Hilda had an idea.
She took out the bin from under
the sink and put Gloria there
instead. Gloria ate all the rubbish!

Now Gloria was happy! She soon
grew a little seed pod.
"Who can we give this seed to?"
said Mia.
"I know!" Zak said.

A month later Zak got another parcel.

Written by Justine Smith • Illustrated by Clare Elsom

All priced at £8.99

Orchard Books are available from all good bookshops,
or can be ordered from our website: www.orchardbooks.co.uk,
or telephone 01235 827702, or fax 01235 827703.

Prices and availability are subject to change.